What Does the Tooth Fairy Do with
All Those Teeth?

by George W. Kelly
Illustrated by Paige Billin-Frye

The C. R. Gibson Company, Norwalk, CT 06856

Most of Georgette's first-grade classmates had been visited by the Tooth Fairy, and Georgette wanted the Tooth Fairy to visit her too.

A new permanent tooth had appeared behind one of her lower front baby teeth. The baby tooth, however, was only slightly wobbly. It showed no signs of falling out. So her mother took her to the dentist Saturday morning.

The dentist "wiggled" out the baby tooth to make room for the new tooth to grow properly in the old space.

Georgette was happy because now she could put the tooth under her pillow for the Tooth Fairy. She knew that the Tooth Fairy would leave a present in exchange for the tooth.

And sure enough, when she woke up on Sunday morning, Georgette found a crisp new dollar bill under her pillow. The tooth was gone.

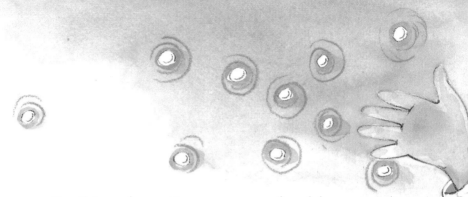

On Monday, Georgette asked her mother, "Mommy, what does the Tooth Fairy do with all those teeth?"

"I don't know for sure," Mommy said, "but I was told that the Tooth Fairy sprinkles them with fairy dust and throws them in the sky. They keep going higher and higher until they get to the Milky Way and turn into tiny white sparkling stars."

"Oh," said Georgette.

On Tuesday, Georgette saw Mrs. Wadsworth who lived next door.

"Mrs. Wadsworth, what does the Tooth Fairy do with all those teeth?" asked Georgette.

"I don't know for sure," said Mrs. Wadsworth, "but I was told that the Tooth Fairy takes them back to Fairy Land, sprinkles fairy dust on them, and uses them to build a magnificent fairy palace. Each tooth is like a tiny block of glistening white marble. The Tooth Fairy never stops building the palace, and it gets bigger and grander each year."

"Oh," said Georgette.

On Wednesday, Georgette saw the mailman, Mr. Giovetti.

"Mr. Giovetti, what does the Tooth Fairy do with all those teeth?" asked Georgette.

"I don't know for sure," Mr. Giovetti said, "but I was told that the Tooth Fairy sprinkles them with fairy dust and scatters them into the ocean. Each tooth is swept away by the waves and then slowly settles to the bottom of the sea where an oyster turns it into a beautiful shiny pearl. That's where pearls come from."

"Oh," said Georgette.

On Thursday, Georgette visited Aunt Dottie.

"Aunt Dottie, what does the Tooth Fairy do with all those teeth?" asked Georgette.

"I don't know for sure," Aunt Dottie said, "but I was told that the Tooth Fairy sprinkles them with fairy dust and hurls them into the darkness of the night. Each tooth disappears, then reappears, over and over again, until you realize it has become a firefly glowing in the dark. That's where fireflies come from."

"Oh," said Georgette.

On Friday, Georgette's grandmother came to Georgette's house.

"Grandma, what does the Tooth Fairy do with all those teeth?" asked Georgette.

"I don't know for sure," Grandma said, "but I was told that the Tooth Fairy sprinkles them with fairy dust and turns each one into a white button, like the buttons on your father's shirt. That's where shirt buttons come from."

"Oh," said Georgette.

On Saturday, Georgette's father took Georgette for a walk in the park.

"Daddy, what does the Tooth Fairy do with all those teeth?" asked Georgette.

"I don't know for sure," Daddy said, "but I was told that the Tooth Fairy sprinkles them with fairy dust and takes them to a workshop in Fairy Land. The fairies hand carve them into little ivory beads. The beads are made into beautiful necklaces. All the fairies love these necklaces and they can never get enough of them."

"Oh," said Georgette.

On Sunday, Georgette went for a playdate to the home of her friend, Elizabeth. Elizabeth had a loose tooth.

"Georgette, do you know what the Tooth Fairy does with all those teeth?" asked Elizabeth.

"Oh yes. I know for sure," answered Georgette. "I asked lots of grown-ups, and they all said the same thing. She sprinkles them with fairy dust, and then she turns them into all the little things all over the world that are bright and sparkly and pearly white—like shirt buttons, fireflies, pearls, and Milky Way stars."

Georgette grinned. "That's what she does with them—you can be sure of that.

"Just ask your mommy."